Captain Flinn
and the
Pirate Dinosaurs
Missing Treasure!

Written by
Giles Andreae

Illustrated by
Russell Ayto

PUFFIN

For ned – G.A.
For my mother and
father – R.A.

A note from the author:

"By the way, there is a dinosaur in this
book called the **giganotosaurus**.
It's a hard word, so it might be a good
idea if you learn how to say it now.
Take it bit by bit . . .

gig – an – OH – toe – SORE – us.

That's it!

Giganotosaurus!"

PUFFIN BOOKS
Published by the Penguin Group: London, New York, Australia, Canada,
India, Ireland, new Zealand and South Africa
Penguin Books Ltd, Registered Offices: 80 Strand, London WC2R 0RL, England
puffinbooks.com
First published 2007
This edition published 2008
1 3 5 7 9 10 8 6 4 2
Text copyright © Giles Andreae, 2007
Illustrations copyright © Russell Ayto, 2007
All rights reserved
The moral right of the author and illustrator has been asserted
Printed in China
ISBN: 978-0-141-50049-2

Flinn's board – KEEP OFF!

This is Flinn. Flinn LOVES dinosaurs.

Tomorrow is a very special day because Flinn's teacher, Miss Pie, is taking his class to see the dinosaur skeletons at the museum.

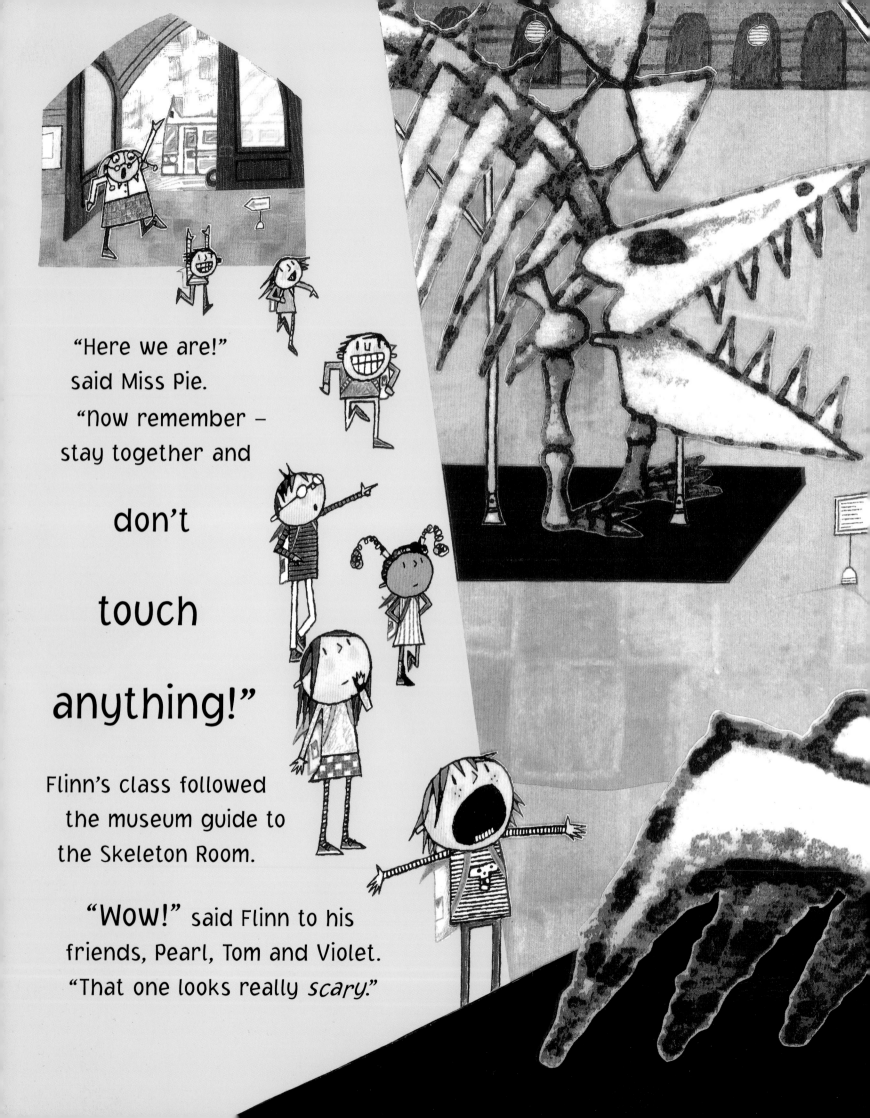

"Here we are!" said Miss Pie. "Now remember – stay together and

don't

touch

anything!"

Flinn's class followed the museum guide to the Skeleton Room.

"Wow!" said Flinn to his friends, Pearl, Tom and Violet. "That one looks really *scary*."

"This is the giganotosaurus,"
said the guide.
"He was even **bigger**
and more **ferocious**
than the **mighty**
Tyrannosaurus Rex."

In the next room, there was a big glass case.
But it was completely EMPTY!

"It used to hold the
treasure of the famous pirate
Captain Rufus Rumblebelly,"
explained the guide,
"but it was **stolen** last night!"

"Real pirate treasure?" said Flinn (who liked pirates
just as much as dinosaurs). "But **who** could have stolen it?"

"Look!" said Tom.
"Maybe these
peculiar feathers
are a clue . . ."

"They seem to be leading to that cupboard," said Pearl.

"Let's follow them!" said Violet.

So Flinn and his friends quietly opened the door and slipped through.

The cupboard was cold
and dark and full of
cobwebs.

"Wait a minute!"
said Flinn. "What's that?"

He bent down
and picked up a
gleaming golden coin.

"And look!
Here's another one."

"It must be the treasure!"
said Violet.

And just at that moment, the back of the cupboard fell away and Flinn and his friends all **tumbled** out . . .

"What treasure?" asked Flinn,
as he quickly untied the pirate.

"Why, the famous treasure of
Rufus Rumblebelly!" said the pirate.
"I'm Gordon Gurgleguts and Rufus
Rumblebelly was my granddaddy.
I took the treasure from the museum –
just to have a little look – but then
someone stole it from me!!"

"That's amazing!" said Flinn.
"We're looking for the treasure too!
We'll help you find it,
but only if you promise
to take it straight
back to the museum."

"All right," said Gurgleguts.
"I promise."

"But who stole it?"
asked Flinn.
"I don't know," said Gurgleguts.
"But I did hear a strange song
as they sailed away.
It went:

'Yo ho ho! ♫

♪ Yo ho ho!

Bag o' Bones Island ♪

♪ ♫ Here we go!'"

"Then that's where **we'll** go!"
said Flinn. "To Bag o' Bones
Island! Come on, everyone!"
"Aye, aye!" said Gurgleguts.
"And why don't YOU be our captain?
Here – take my hat."

So Captain Flinn took the helm and they swiftly set sail for Bag o' Bones Island.

"Island ahoy!" shouted Pirate Violet from the crow's nest.

"Follow me, everyone," said Captain Flinn. "There's thick jungle ahead and we don't want anyone to get lost . . ."

"Gurgleguts? Gurgleguts?"

"WHERE ARE YOU?"

"Wait," said Pirate Pearl. "What's that noise?"

In front of them was a clearing. Captain Flinn peered into it and shuddered.
"Pirates!" he said. "But they're not just ordinary pirates. They're . . .

"...PIRATE DINOSAURS!"
And he was right!
There was . . .

A PIRATE DIPLODOCUS . . .

A PIRATE STEGOSAURUS . . .

A PIRATE TRICERATOPS . . .

AND A GREAT BIG PIRATE
TYRANNOSAURUS REX.

Beside the Pirate Dinosaurs
was a huge pile of gleaming
treasure. And next to the
treasure, tied up from head
to foot, was Gurgleguts.

The Pirate Dinosaurs were singing a terrible son

"We've stolen all the treasure
We'll use it at our leisure
And won't it be a pleasure
For us all to live like kings!

"And don't think we've forgotten
That this pirate's rather rotten
So let's barbecue his bottom
With some spicy chicken wings!"

"Stop!" yelled Captain Flinn.
"Untie my friend **immediately!**"

"We couldn't possibly do that,"
said the Tyrannosaurus Rex,
squeezing a huge dollop of
tomato ketchup on to Gurgleguts' head.
"Because we're going to

EAT HIM UP!"

"Well then, you slimy seafaring sausages,"
said Captain Flinn, drawing his cutlass,
"you nasty *noodle-brained* nincompoops,
you dirty *dastardly* dunderheads—
you're going to have to

eat

me

first!

ATTACK!"

Crash!

Suddenly, Captain Flinn took a huge **swipe** at the Tyrannosaurus Rex, and **pinned** him up against a tree.

"Please spare me," said the Tyrannosaurus Rex, "and I promise to be the goodest goody in the whole world . . . EVER."

"You great **big fibber!**" said Captain Flinn.
"Fibber, eh?" said the Tyrannosaurus Rex angrily.
"Well then, I think it's time you met my cousin!"

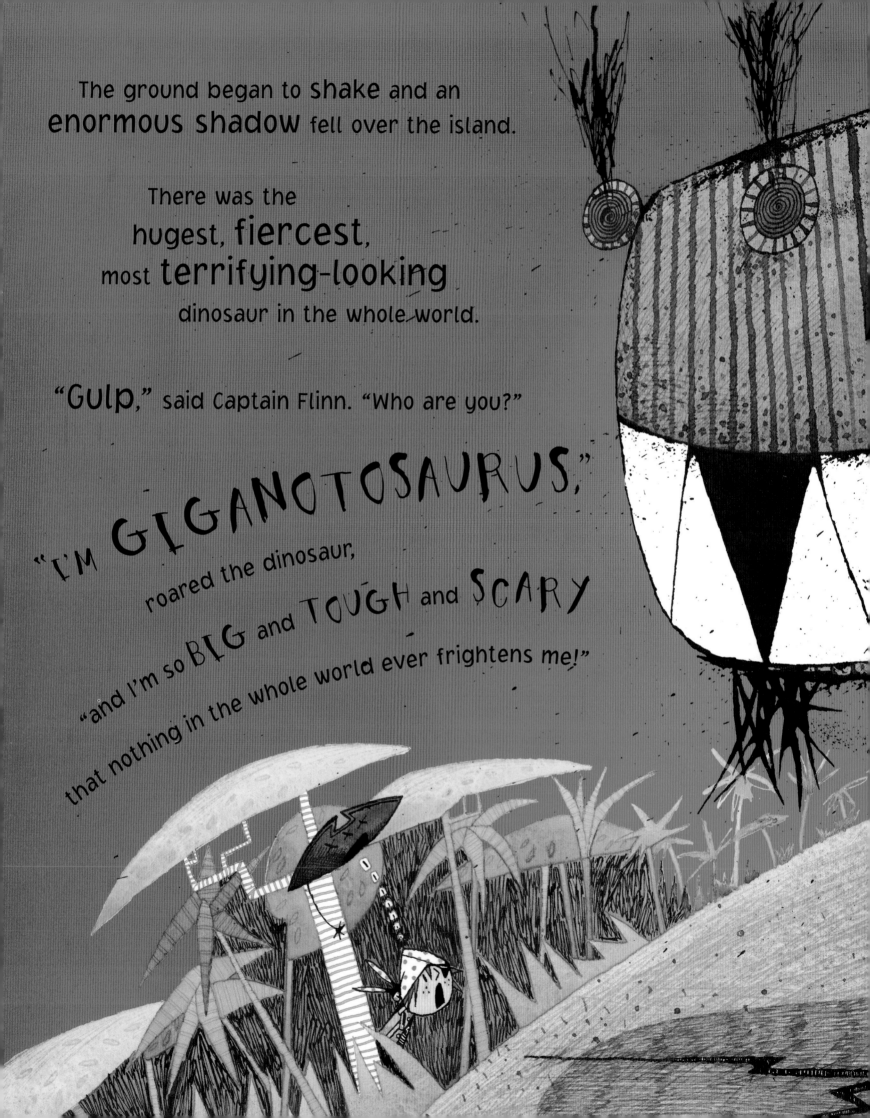

The ground began to **shake** and an **enormous shadow** fell over the island.

There was the
hugest, **fiercest**,
most **terrifying-looking**
dinosaur in the whole world.

"Gulp," said Captain Flinn. "Who are you?"

"I'M GIGANOTOSAURUS,"
roared the dinosaur,
"and I'm so BIG and TOUGH and SCARY
that nothing in the whole world ever frightens me!"

Then suddenly . . .

"Well, shiver me timbers," said Flinn. "Fancy a big old dinosaur being scared of a teeny-weeny spider!"

HHH!"

cried the Giganotosaurus.

"Spider! Spider! Help! HEEEELP!!"

A tiny spider was hanging from Captain Flinn's pirate hat.

"They're just so creepy and crawly," wailed the Giganotosaurus.
"Keep him away from me – please!"

In all the commotion, Captain Flinn saw his chance.

He quickly freed Gurgleguts and,
in a flash, all the Pirate Dinosaurs AND
the Giganotosaurus were tightly tied up.

Then Captain Flinn picked up the treasure.
"Quick, gang," he said, "let's get back
to the ship. It's time to go home."
And off they all sailed.

"LAND AHOY!" cried Violet.

So the children hugged Gurgleguts goodbye,

then,
one
by
one,
they clambered
through the ship

into the open cupboard . . .

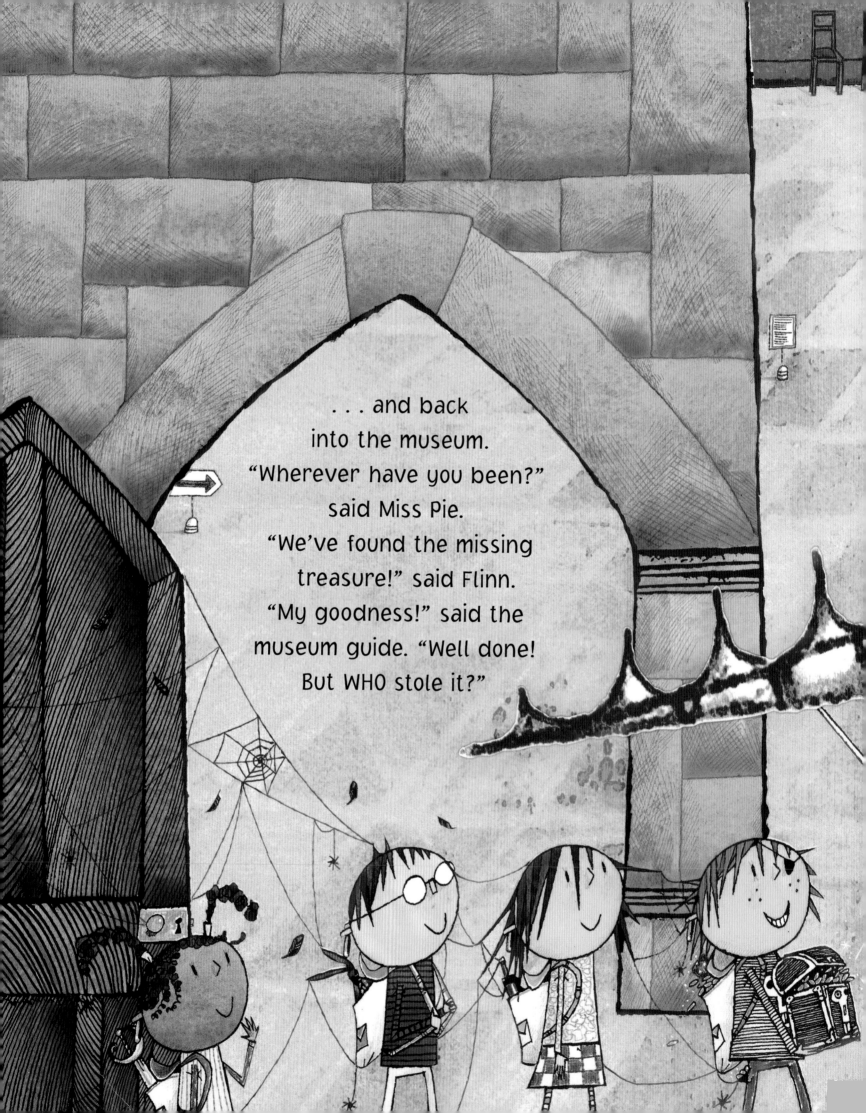

. . . and back
into the museum.
"Wherever have you been?"
said Miss Pie.
"We've found the missing
treasure!" said Flinn.
"My goodness!" said the
museum guide. "Well done!
But WHO stole it?"

"It's a long story," said Flinn. "But it ended up in the hands of some pirates. Oh, and they weren't just pirates, they were PIRATE DINOSAURS!"

"Pirate Dinosaurs!" laughed the guide. "That's the silliest thing I've heard in my whole life! Pirate Dinosaurs indeed!"

"And just for your information," added Flinn, "I can tell you something about your giganotosaurus. He was **frightened** of **spiders**. Very frightened indeed."